FERNO VS EPOS

Special thanks to Edward Willet

To Alice, my warrior princess

www.beastquest.co.uk

ORCHARD BOOKS
338 Euston Road, London NW1 3BH
Orchard Books Australia
Level 17/207 Kent St, Sydney, NSW 2000

A Paperback Original
First published in Great Britain in 2012

Beast Quest is a registered trademark of Beast Quest Limited
Series created by Beast Quest Limited, London

Text © Beast Quest Limited 2012
Cover and inside illustrations by Steve Sims © Orchard Books 2012

A CIP catalogue record for this book is available from
the British Library.

ISBN 978 1 40831 867 6

3 5 7 9 10 8 6 4

Printed and bound by CPI Group (UK) Ltd, Croydon, CR0 4YY

The paper and board used in this paperback are natural recyclable
products made from wood grown in sustainable forests. The
manufacturing processes conform to the environmental regulations of
the country of origin.

Orchard Books is a division of Hachette Children's Books,
an Hachette UK company

www.hachette.co.uk

FERNO vs EPOS

BY ADAM BLADE

ORCHARD

THE ICY P

THE NORTHERN
MOUNTAINS

THE O

WESTERN OCEAN

THE FOREST
OF FEAR

THE

Greetings, Sam of Littleton!

Word has reached me of your bravery.
Are you ready to become a hero?

I am Tom, Master of the Beasts. It
is my duty to protect Avantia. But
evil never sleeps, and I travel from
east to west, north to south, keeping
our enemies at bay. So, to help me, I
have decided to create a new band of
Knights. I want you to be one of them!

Ride swiftly to King Hugo's Palace.
There, you will join my Knight
Academy, where you will learn the
art of combat — and the secrets of
the Beasts.

Avantia is counting on you!

Tom

PART ONE

THE KNIGHT ACADEMY

CHAPTER ONE

A GATHERING OF RECRUITS

"Look, Warrior," said Sam, patting his shire horse on the neck. "We made it!"

Ahead, the walls of the City loomed above him. Crowds of people streamed in and out of the gate, some driving carts laden with vegetables, some carrying baskets of bread. An old woman leading a goat smiled up at Sam. "If you carry on gaping like that, you'll catch a fly!" she called.

Sam grinned back. He'd never seen anything as big as the City before. It couldn't be more different from his village of Littleton, near the Grassy Plains. Sam nudged Warrior gently in the ribs, and his horse obediently clip-clopped forward. He patted Warrior's neck.

"Good boy!" Sam was proud of his steed. Warrior hadn't hesitated once during the two-day ride, though he was far more used to pulling a plough than carrying a rider across half of Avantia.

The *thud-thud-thud* of Warrior's
hooves changed to a loud clatter as
the packed dirt of the road gave way
to cobblestones. There were people
everywhere, selling or buying bread,
cheese and fruit from little stalls. Sam
looked around for someone to ask
for directions. A young red-haired

Armoury→

Finest→
Live Stock

City Gates←

woman selling meat pies smiled at him, so he guided Warrior over to her stall. "Can you direct me to the palace?" he said.

The woman laughed. "Are you looking for work?"

No, I'm going there to become a Knight, Sam wanted to tell her. But he was afraid she wouldn't believe him. "In a way," he said.

"Well, you can't miss it," the woman replied. "This road will take you right there."

Sam thanked her. He felt a grin splitting his face. He really was in the City. And he really was going to become a Knight of Avantia!

I wish Lisbeth could see this, he thought. He missed his big sister, who had raised him since he was just a baby, after their parents died from a fever. She had been by his side when a fierce-looking Knight in gilded chainmail arrived in Littleton, bearing an ornate scroll with Sam's name on it. Sam had read the message on it many times, but he still couldn't believe it. Nor could anyone in their village.

In the City, each turn revealed a new wonder: a white marble fountain, a rose garden with a fragrance that filled the surrounding streets, a street puppeteer entertaining a group of children. He could still hear their laughter as he turned one last corner – and his mouth dropped open in wonder.

King Hugo's palace stood in the middle of an enormous park. Tall towers rose from the roof, from which bright blue pennants fluttered.

Sam rode up to the open gate,
where two guards stood to attention,
their armour gleaming in the sun.
They watched Sam approach with
expressionless faces.

"Halt," said one of the guards.
"State your business."

Sam reined in Warrior. Heart pounding, he reached inside his jerkin for Tom's scroll. *What if it's all a mistake?* he thought. *What if I'm not really supposed to be here?*

He held out the scroll to the guard, who took it and read the text. "Sam of Littleton," he said, with the ghost of a smile. "Welcome to King Hugo's Palace! The Master is expecting you. I'll take you to him."

Sam slid off Warrior's back, excitement tingling inside him as they went through the palace gate. A young man came running to take Warrior's reins.

"He'll look after your horse," the guard said.

Sam handed the reins to the youth, before following the guard in the opposite direction.

They crossed the wide courtyard to an archway that led into another, smaller yard. A row of red and white targets hung on a huge stack of hay bales pushed up against the palace wall. At the other end of the courtyard, an archway three times as tall as Sam led deeper into the palace. Carved into the stone were six images – a dragon, a sea serpent, a giant, a man with a horse's body and legs, a monster covered in shaggy hair, and a giant bird.

The Good Beasts of Avantia, Sam thought. His mother used to tell him stories about how they protected the kingdom.

Other boys and girls stood in small groups around the courtyard. They were talking together, but fell silent when they spotted Sam.

"Wait here," the guard told him, and headed back to the palace gate.

A girl waved at Sam. "Come and join us!" she called. She had pale blonde hair and bright blue eyes, and fixed Sam with a friendly smile.

Sam walked over to her and the boy she was with.

"You must be Sam," the girl said, and held out her hand. "I'm Zora."

Sam shook it.

"And I'm Will," said the boy. He had dark skin and gleaming brown eyes. "Where are you from? My home's a fishing village on the Western Ocean."

"I'm from Littleton," Sam said. "It's—"

But then everyone fell silent as a newcomer strode into the courtyard. He looked to be a few years older than Sam. He wore a sword, hung on a belt of red leather. Strapped to his left arm was a shield bearing six tokens: a dragon scale, a serpent's tooth, an eagle's feather, a piece of a horseshoe, a golden bell, and a talon.

Sam's breath caught in his throat. Tom himself! Everyone in the kingdom had heard about Tom's Quests. The Master of the Beasts was said to have saved Avantia many, many times.

And now he was standing just a few paces away from Sam!

"Welcome to the Knight Academy," Tom said. His face was stern as he looked around at them. "You are not here to enjoy yourselves. You are here to learn to serve your kingdom. Remember, evil never sleeps. It must be fought at every turn."

Sam felt a small fire of determination

glow inside him. He knew
instinctively that he would do
whatever Tom needed him to do.

Tom held his grim look for a
moment, glancing from face to face.
But then he grinned. "It's time for
you to become heroes of Avantia!"

CHAPTER TWO

SWORD SKILLS

"Before we start your training," Tom told the recruits, "there's somebody else you need to meet."

He stepped to one side, and a girl came out of the archway behind him. As tall as Tom, she had short, spiky hair and carried a bow. The feathered ends of arrows peeked over her back from a full quiver.

"This is Elenna," Tom said. "My best

friend, who has fought alongside me on all of my Quests."

"Welcome," Elenna said, her eyes sweeping over the group of Knights-to-be. "I look forward to teaching you. You will need all the knowledge, skill and bravery you can muster in the Quests that lie ahead."

Tom nodded in agreement. "I have personally selected each of you to be among the first to study in my new Knight Academy," he said, "because you have shown enormous bravery in helping or protecting others."

He stepped into the group, and put a hand on Sam's shoulder. "Sam here," he said, "defeated a pack of hyenas – all by himself." Sam felt his face grow hot at being singled out. He couldn't work out how Tom had heard the story of his battle against a hyena pack that had slipped into Littleton's market, sending everyone screaming. Even though he had only been armed with a shepherd's crook and a small blade, Sam had stood his ground against the creatures and driven them out of the market.

Everyone in Littleton knew the story – but Sam had not expected it to reach as far as the City.

Then Tom nodded towards Zora. "Zora risked her life climbing a mountain on a stormy night, to take medicine to a sick old woman."

Zora turned bright red and looked down at her feet.

Tom turned to Will, who froze in place as the Master of the Beasts gripped his shoulder. "Will swam out to sea to rescue a drowning dog that had fallen off a fishing boat."

"I like dogs," Will murmured, and everyone laughed.

Soon Tom had mentioned all of the recruits, except one – a tall boy, closer to Tom's age than Sam's. Sam watched him slipping around in the crowd, somehow never being in the right place for Tom to single him out.

He must be shy, Sam thought.

He wondered what the boy's name was. He had sallow skin and lank, shoulder-length hair that was as pale as the worms Sam found under logs back home. When he caught Sam looking at him, he glared back with eyes as murky as a stagnant pool. Sam looked away. *So he isn't shy*, thought Sam. *So why does he keep trying to hide?*

At Tom's command, servants emerged from the archway carrying trays of bread, ham and apples, as well as flagons of water. When the recruits had eaten, Elenna handed each of them a wooden sword, keeping one for herself.

"Now your training to become a Knight begins," Tom said. He drew his sword from its sheath, and swung it at Elenna in a sweeping arc. She lunged forwards, blocking Tom's attack with the wooden blade.

"It all begins with balance," Tom said. "Watch how Elenna keeps her feet braced."

He thrust his sword at Elenna again. She stepped to the right, supporting her weight with both feet, and swung her weapon at Tom's. Their blades clashed.

"If you're off-balance, your opponent can knock you over," Tom went on. "I'm going to show you how quickly you'll lose the fight if that happens."

Tom retreated a few paces from Elenna. Then, raising his sword, he charged. Elenna waited, her knees bent into a crouch, bouncing lightly on the balls of her feet. When Tom reached her, she twisted to one side.

Tom staggered. Elenna swung her sword, the wooden blade whistling through the air. It smacked into Tom's sword. He kept hold of his blade but his foot slipped, and he landed on his knees on the flagstones.

"Surrender, Tom!" Elenna said. Then she grinned and reached out a hand to help him up.

Tom looked around at the recruits. "Now it's your turn. Everybody pair up and we'll see what you can do."

Voices rang out as the recruits paired up. Sam noticed that the strange-looking boy was by himself, his eyes darting uneasily around the others. *Now's my chance to find out what he's up to*, Sam thought.

He went over to the boy. "Do you want to be my fighting partner?" he asked, trying to sound as friendly as possible.

The boy's face twisted into a crooked smile. "Are you sure you want to be mine?"

Before Sam could answer, Tom yelled, "Begin!" All around the courtyard, the recruits lunged at each other, swords clacking noisily.

The boy swung his wooden blade.

Sam blocked it, but the boy had used so much force that Sam's arms shuddered all the way up to his shoulders.

"You're stronger than you look," gasped Sam, as he swung his wooden sword at the boy. "Where did you learn to fight like that?"

The boy shrugged. "Nowhere. I grew up on a farm, just like you."

Sam lunged at him. Their blades clashed, forming a cross shape. Sam gritted his teeth, leaning with all his strength to try to take control of the fight. The boy did the same. Both his hands were clenched around the hilt of his sword. Sam noticed that they were squeezed white with the effort – and were as soft and smooth as a baby's.

He's never worked on a farm in his life, Sam thought, *or his hands would be rough like mine. But why would he lie?*

Tom called out for the recruits to pause for a moment. Sam and the strange boy stepped away from each other.

He's got a secret, Sam decided. *And I'm going to find out what it is.*

CHAPTER THREE

A DARING THEFT

The following morning, Sam and
the other recruits emerged from the
barracks where they had spent the
night. Tom and Elenna were waiting
in the palace courtyard.

"We've got something special to
show you," Tom said. "This way!"

They went through the archway
that led into the palace and down
a winding staircase. Tom and Elenna

halted outside an ironbound door, with torches burning on either side of it.

"The Palace Armoury," Elenna said. She knocked.

The door swung open to reveal a young man in long blue robes. His brown eyes twinkled in the torchlight. In his right hand he held a long staff of white wood carved

with intricate patterns.

"This is Daltec, a Good Wizard of Avantia," Tom told the students. "He has been looking after the armoury since the Master of Arms retired."

"Follow me," Daltec told the recruits. "I'll give you the grand tour."

The recruits followed him down a long corridor. Sam glanced over his shoulder to see the strange boy lingering several paces behind.

"He makes me shiver," Zora whispered. "When he looks at you, it's like being turned to ice."

Sam nodded. "Let's keep an eye on him."

Daltec led them past racks of swords, shelves of helmets and a whole room lined with glittering suits of armour. Deeper in the armoury, the wizard showed them mystical weapons that once belonged to great heroes – and some that had belonged to fearsome villains.

Daltec pointed to a round shield of beaten silver. "This was the shield of Taladon, Tom's father."

Sam's eyes slid from the shining shield to a black-handled scythe with a dark, pitted blade. Sam gasped, remembering one of the stories the smith in Littleton had told him. "Is that...?"

"The scythe of Mortaxe the Skeleton Warrior," Daltec confirmed gravely. "A weapon Tom once faced in battle."

Tom shuddered. "A weapon that almost ended my Quests!"

Daltec smiled. "But it didn't."

They walked on, reaching another

closed door. It was sheathed in dark iron and held fast by three locks.

"Beyond this door," Daltec said, "are the kingdom's greatest treasures." He pulled a ring of keys from his belt and opened the locks, one after the other.

Behind him, Sam heard the pale boy's breathing quicken. He glanced over his shoulder. *What's wrong with him?*

Daltec pushed open the door. Torches sprang magically to life. Sam gasped again as he stepped into the room. Its floor, walls and domed ceiling were all made of smooth white marble. On a raised dais, a suit of armour hung on a stand, glittering in the torchlight.

"This," Daltec said, "is the Golden Armour." He pointed with his staff.

"The helmet gives the wearer the eyesight of an eagle. The chainmail provides strength of heart. The breastplate increases his physical strength. The leg armour gives him great speed and endurance when running, and the boots help him leap impossible distances. Finally," he said, pointing at the metal gloves, "the gauntlets make him one of the deadliest swordsmen in all the known worlds." His staff swung toward Tom. "And as Master of the Beasts, Tom has all of these abilities even when he's not wearing the armour."

As one, the recruits turned to look at Tom, who smiled.

"Show us, Tom!" Will called out.

Tom shook his head. "The powers aren't for showing off," he said. "They're for use only when there is great need."

"Well, I really need to see you

use them," Will said, and everyone laughed.

Tom raised his hands, chuckling. "All right. Maybe just a small demonstration." He looked around. Four chairs, carved from solid marble, rested at regular intervals around the walls. He walked over to the nearest one, and then crouched to grip one of the chair's legs. He stood up, holding the heavy stone seat in one hand, as though it weighed no more than a loaf of bread.

"The power of the breastplate," he told them.

Everyone cheered – or almost everyone. Sam glanced back, but he couldn't see the tall, pale boy any more. Sam quickly scanned the room and saw that he had moved off to one side. His eyes were on Tom, but he was easing away from the group, each slow step taking him closer to the Golden Armour at the centre of the room.

What's he up to? Sam wondered, puzzled.

The pale boy was now right in front of the central dais. Suddenly he spun and reached out for the Armour.

"Hey!" Sam shouted.

Everyone looked around. The pale boy snatched the gauntlets from the armour stand, then whirled to face them all, a triumphant smirk on his face.

"Put those back!" Sam cried.

"Make me," the pale boy sneered.

Sam dashed forward, but the boy raised his right hand and fired a bolt of black lightning from his palm. It

slammed into Sam's chest like a giant
fist, sending him skidding backwards
across the smooth marble floor. He
crashed into the feet of the other
recruits, upending them.

"Fool," the pale boy snarled.
"Do you dare to challenge me?"

"I challenge you," said Tom,
drawing his sword. "But first,
tell me who you are."

If the boy was frightened, it didn't show in his arrogant face. His cold voice was as steady as Tom's sword-arm. "I am Maximus, son of the greatest Dark Wizard of all time – Malvel! My father may be dead, but his power lives on in me – and now I will use it to make Avantia suffer!"

CHAPTER FOUR

A NEW HERO

Tom wasted no more time on words.
He charged the dais – only to be sent
flying back by another bolt of magic
from Maximus's palm. As Elenna and
Daltec bounded forwards, readying
their own weapons, the evil young
wizard cast lightning bolts at them.

Before Avantia's three heroes and
their students could regain their
feet, Maximus had dashed out of the

47

door, taking the gauntlets with him.

"After him!" Tom cried. He led Elenna, Daltec and the recruits in a chase. Their footsteps clattered up the winding stairs and back down the long corridors to the training courtyard.

At the archway, Maximus stopped and glanced back. "The first to catch me is the first to die!" he shouted, and flung another bolt of dark magic, which just missed Sam's head. A suit

of armour standing against the wall exploded in a storm of shattered metal.

Laughing, Maximus dashed outside.

Tom burst past the recruits and made it to the archway first. Sam was close behind him, emerging just in time to see Maximus run to the middle of the courtyard.

With a yell of determination, Tom charged the Boy Wizard. But as he swung his blade, Maximus vanished in a black flash, leaving behind only a puff of foul-smelling smoke.

Tom pulled up short. Elenna and Daltec joined him, their eyes scanning the empty yard. "Search the Palace!" Tom shouted.

Sam whirled around, and a flash of movement caught his eye.

"There!" he said, pointing towards one of the Palace walls.

Maximus was perched on the top, looking down at them. He held the gauntlets out in front of him, one in each hand. Black flames flickered around them as he snarled a curse, his voice ringing in the courtyard:

"Come, cruel magic of Malvel,
Fill these gauntlets with your spell.
Lure two Beasts to deadly battle,
Make them fight with tooth and claw,
'Til one Beast lives and one draws
breath no more."

Maximus's voice seemed to freeze Sam's blood. The Good Beasts protected Avantia. If Maximus forced them to destroy each other, the kingdom would be in terrible danger!

Maximus laughed – a terrible, mocking sound. Filled with fury, Sam grabbed one of the wooden training swords from the ground and flung it as hard as he could at the Boy Wizard.

The sword fell short, but the suddenness of the attack startled Maximus. By reflex, he threw his left arm across his face – and in that

moment, Daltec raised his staff.
A bolt of white lightning struck
Maximus's shoulder. He staggered.
The gauntlet dropped from his
grasp. Tom leapt forwards and
caught it before it smashed onto the
cobblestones.

"Your curse is broken, Maximus!"
Daltec shouted. "Return the other
gauntlet and we will let you leave
in peace!"

Maximus's face had twisted in
fury, but now his mocking sneer
returned. "Do you really think the
loss of one gauntlet is enough to stop
my curse?" he shouted. He held out
his remaining gauntlet. "I can still
control a Beast with this one. And
I will use that Beast to attack the
others."

He pointed down at the gauntlet

in Tom's hand. Black flames flickered
around it again. Tom grimaced in
pain, but he held on to it.

"And know this, Master of Beasts,"
Maximus snarled. "The gauntlet
you still have will do you no good.
For I have cursed it further – from
this day on, it can only be worn
by an untested warrior. Someone
who can't possibly stand against
the might of my magic!" He jerked
his hand back and the black flames
vanished. "Choose your champion!
And let him face the first Beast I will
command – Ferno the Fire Dragon!"

Sam grabbed another wooden
sword to hurl at Maximus, but the
Boy Wizard had vanished before
he could take aim. Black smoke
wavered in the shape of his outline
for a moment, and then blew away

in the morning breeze.

Sam looked around at the other recruits. Their faces were pale with horror.

"If Maximus forces the Beasts to fight, they will destroy each other!" Zora whispered.

"And then Avantia will be at his mercy!" Will moaned.

Daltec raised his hands for quiet. "All is not lost!" He pointed at the metal glove in Tom's hand. "We still have one gauntlet. What we need is a hero to wear it and tame a Beast. Who will ride a Beast against Ferno? Who will prevent a fight to the death between two Good Beasts of Avantia?"

Tom, grim-faced, held up his hand to stop anyone from stepping forward. "I am the Master of the

Beasts," he said sternly. "This Quest
is mine."

"Tom," said Elenna, stepping
towards her friend. "You can't.
Maximus's curse—"

"It's my duty," Tom said. Then his
expression softened into a confident

smile. "Besides, just because Maximus said he put a curse on the gauntlet does not mean he actually did. If he is anything like his father, he is probably a liar."

Sam saw Elenna frown, a look of uncertainty on her face. But Daltec bowed. "It is yours to try, of course."

Holding the gauntlet in his right hand, Tom started to slide it onto his left – but the moment the gauntlet touched his left hand, the metal glove snapped into a tightly clenched fist, crushing Tom's fingers. Tom gasped in pain, then held the gauntlet carefully by the wrist-guard.

He looked around at the recruits. "It seems Maximus was telling the truth after all," he said quietly. "This Quest is not meant for me. We need a new hero."

A tall, heavily-muscled boy brushed past Sam. "I'll do it!"

Tom handed him the gauntlet, but the boy fell to his knees as if he had been handed the heaviest boulder in Avantia. He tried to lift it, his muscles straining.

"It's too heavy," he said, getting up and wiping the sweat from his forehead.

"I'll try," said a girl with short black hair. She reached down to pick up the gauntlet, but no sooner had she touched it than she yelped and jumped back, blowing on her fingers. "It burns!"

As he watched, Sam felt a strange sense of power flow through him, as though his blood had been replaced by liquid fire. His ears buzzed and his own voice sounded distant as he

stepped forward and said, "Let
me try."

Tom gestured at the gauntlet,
which still lay on the cobblestones.

Sam knelt and picked it up.
It wasn't heavy. It didn't burn. It
looked far too big for his hand, but
when he slipped his fingers inside, it
shrank until it fitted him perfectly.

Sam stared at the gauntlet, flexing his gold-sheathed fingers. The strange magical feeling still coursed through his veins.

"The gauntlet of the Golden Armour has chosen Sam as its champion," said Tom solemnly. He stepped forward and raised Sam's gauntleted hand high over his head. "Congratulations, Sam of Littleton – Avantia's newest hero!"

CHAPTER FIVE

SWORD AND SHIELD

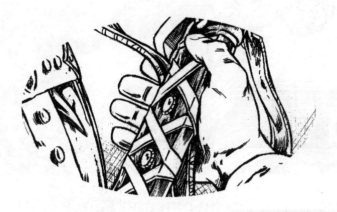

A short time later, Sam stood inside Tom's private chambers, high up in one of the palace's towers. Tom was pulling a thick book, bound in red leather, from a tall bookcase stuffed with ancient tomes and scrolls of dusty parchment. He lugged the heavy book to a desk beneath one of the windows. Elenna and Daltec

gathered beside him and Sam joined
them. The title of the book was
written in gold lettering: *The Complete
Book of Beasts*.

"This book," Tom told Sam,
"contains everything we know about
all the Beasts of Avantia – and the
other known realms, too. You must
use it to choose which Beast you will
ride against Maximus and Ferno."

Sam hoped Tom didn't notice his hands trembling as he opened the heavy red cover and began turning the pages. Each bore a beautiful drawing of a Beast, painted in brilliant colours and gilded with silver and gold. The pictures were so detailed it looked as though they might leap off the page. Descriptions beneath the drawings listed the Beasts' powers and history. On one page, Ferno breathed golden fire at Sam, and he turned it hurriedly. He saw Sepron the Sea Serpent, Arcta the Mountain Giant, Tagus the Horse-Man, and many, many others.

How can I possibly choose? Sam wondered.

Tom and Daltec had moved to one corner of the room, where they spoke in low voices. Elenna was still close by, watching Sam.

"Think about it logically," she said. "Forget about your Beast for the moment. Think about the one Maximus will be riding."

Sam flipped back to Ferno's frightening picture.

"What are Ferno's special powers?" Elenna asked.

"You mean apart from being big enough to swallow me in one gulp?" Sam said.

Elenna grinned. "Yes. Apart from that."

Sam looked at the text underneath the dragon's picture. "He can fly and breathe fire."

"Right," Elenna said. "So you'll need a Beast that can stand up to such attacks."

Sam nodded slowly and searched

through the pages again. He hesitated, and then flipped back. "I think I've found the Beast that can fight Ferno."

"Well?" Tom said, as he approached the desk.

Sam pointed to a drawing of a magnificent phoenix rising from the flaming crater of a volcano, wings spread, golden beak agape. "This one – Epos the Flame Bird."

"Why?" Tom asked.

"She can fly," Sam answered, "so I'll be able to meet Ferno and Maximus in the air. And she can create balls of flame between her talons. I can fight fire with fire."

Tom placed a hand on Sam's shoulder. "An excellent choice."

Daltec took a long leather tube from the top shelf of the overflowing bookcase. He opened one end and slid out a roll of parchment. Tom moved the book aside so Daltec could spread the parchment on the desk. Sam gasped. It was a map of Avantia, so beautifully drawn and detailed he felt almost as if he were already flying on Epos, looking down at the kingdom.

Daltec held his hands out above the map, murmuring in a low voice. White sparks danced around his fingertips.

A spell, Sam thought.

Two glowing images appeared on the map – tiny drawings of Ferno and Epos. Sam bent closer. Epos's image was on top of a volcano, and Ferno's was inside his mountain lair far to the south.

How long will it take Maximus to reach the Fire Dragon? he wondered. *I must tame Epos in time to fight him. I'll worry about getting into the volcano once I'm there*, Sam told himself. *It is all up to me now.*

His thoughts were interrupted by Tom. "I have something for you, too," he said. Going to the foot of his bed, he lifted the lid of a wooden chest and took out a sword in a silver and black scabbard, and a large round shield. He brought them to Sam.

"These weapons once belonged to my mother," Tom explained. He held out the shield so Sam could slip his left arm through the straps.

At first Sam thought the shield was made of ordinary metal, but when Tom lifted it, its shining surface was suddenly frosted with ice. The next instant, the frost was chased away by a sheet of liquid fire. The fire burned and crackled for just a moment, before the shield's face returned to its dull, metallic grey.

"It's amazing," breathed Sam.

Tom nodded. "The surface changes according to the danger you face."

Then Tom handed him the sword. Holding the scabbard in his left hand, which still wore the magical gauntlet from the Golden Armour, Sam drew the blade with his right. The sword

hissed like an angry snake. Sam turned
it this way and that, the light from the
windows glittering along its length,
then slipped it back into its sheath
and buckled it around his waist.

"You look like a great warrior,"
Elenna said.

Fierce determination flooded Sam.
I'm going on a real adventure!

He would not fail. He would tame
a Beast, face Maximus in battle and
stop Ferno and Epos from fighting
to the death.

I have to. If I don't, no one else will.

At dawn the following day, Sam
heaved his saddle onto Warrior's
broad back. As he tightened the straps,
he thought about what lay ahead of
him, and his tiredness faded away.

The other recruits stood around the courtyard, their faces pale in the pre-dawn light.

Sam turned to face Tom, Elenna and Daltec. "I'm ready," he told them. And he meant it. The magical shield hung on his back, the golden gauntlet was snug on his left hand, while his right wore an ordinary leather riding glove. In the Armoury, Daltec had found him a leather jacket studded with iron rings, which he wore with his own patched black trousers and boots.

"Not quite ready!" said a voice behind him. He turned to see Will holding a cloth-wrapped bundle and a flask. "Food and water for the journey."

Zora stepped up beside Will. "Promise you'll come back safely, Sam," she said. "I want to hear all about your Quest!"

"I promise," Sam said, but he had a knot in his stomach – he knew it wasn't a promise he could be sure of keeping.

He tucked the food and water into his saddlebags. Then he mounted Warrior. Will and Zora went back to join the other recruits. Tom, who had been watching silently, stepped forwards and put his hand on the bridle.

"Nervous?" Tom asked.

"A bit," Sam admitted.

Tom smiled. "I was too, on my first Quest."

"Really?" Sam said, surprised.

"Terrified, actually," Tom admitted. "But I knew I couldn't let that stop me. The Quest was mine, and only I could complete it. Just like this Quest is yours." He extended a hand for

Sam to shake. "While there is blood
in my veins, I'm certain you have
the courage to win this Quest – and
become a Knight of Avantia!"

Sam felt the knot in his stomach
dissolve as he grasped Tom's hand.
"And as long as blood flows in my

veins, too," he swore, "I won't let you down!"

Tom stepped back. "Then go, Sam of Littleton. Fulfil your Quest!"

Sam saluted him by clapping his fist against his heart. Then he rode out of the Palace, the cheers of his fellow recruits echoing through the courtyard.

He urged Warrior to a canter, then to a gallop.

I must not fail in my Quest, he thought. *Avantia is depending on me!*

CHAPTER SIX

THE CHIEFTAIN'S DAUGHTER

Warrior trotted along a narrow mountain path, trailing a long shadow.

"Whoa, boy," Sam said, pulling on the reins.

The big horse stopped, stamping his feet and blowing. Sam stood up in the stirrups to study the deep, forested valley that opened up in front of

them. In the distance was a strange,
flat-topped mountain from which
poured a cloud of grey ash, tinged
red by mighty fires just out of sight.

Epos's lair, Sam thought. *The great
volcano of the east.*

A jet of flame burst from the crater,
briefly taking the shape of a fiery
mushroom. Sam saw a stream of lava
course down a narrow gully in the

mountain's side. He frowned. How
could he possibly get inside it to
find Epos?

Sam pulled out the magical map.
He remembered seeing a town
marked somewhere nearby, and
sure enough, a cluster of houses was
drawn near the volcano's base. Its
name was scrawled in tiny letters.

"Stonewin," Sam read aloud. He

looked up. The path dipped down into the valley a short distance ahead. According to the map, it would take him straight to Stonewin. "Maybe someone there will know of a safe way into the crater," he said to Warrior. The horse flicked an ear, but didn't take his eyes off the volcano.

Sam couldn't blame him.

He tucked the map away and jerked the reins. Warrior balked, obviously unwilling to go closer to the strange, fiery mountain. "Come on, boy," Sam murmured. "We don't have a choice." His faithful horse whinnied, but trotted down into the valley.

It was still daylight when Sam and Warrior reached Stonewin, but a deep shadow seemed to hang across the land. The plume of smoke and ash had thickened, making it difficult to see very far ahead, and Sam could hear a constant low rumbling. Every now and then the ground shook beneath Warrior's hooves, making the big horse move from side to side uneasily.

The volcano's stirring, Sam thought grimly. *We need to find Epos before it erupts.*

Stonewin was in chaos. People rushed along the streets, putting up shutters, covering chimneys with tall peaked caps of tin. Some herded cows and sheep and horses into slate-roofed barns.

An old woman was nailing wooden boards over the windows of her hut. She stared at Sam with wide eyes.

"We don't have much time," she cried. "If the wind shifts, we'll be buried in ash!"

Sam guided Warrior over to her.
"I need to get inside the volcano.
Do you know—"

"Are you blind?" The old woman
pointed at the billowing grey cloud.
"The volcano is erupting! You need to
take cover, lad!" She turned her back
and hurried into her hut. The door
slammed shut.

Sam trotted Warrior over to a
young man with a squawking chicken
under each arm, but when he tried to
talk to him, the young man snapped,
"No time! No time!" and brushed past
him to run down an alley.

Everyone was too distracted to help
him. He rode on to the edge of town.
There he saw one person who had
remained calm. Not far ahead of him,
a girl about his age was wrestling
with a white mare. The horse jerked

her head as though she would break free and bolt at any moment. The girl held tightly to the bridle, and was whispering to her.

Sam rode closer. "Why aren't you sealing up your house like everyone else?"

"Because my servants will do that for me," said the girl. "What's it to you, anyway?"

She tossed her long hair over her shoulder and went back to trying to soothe the terrified mare. Sam noticed that Warrior seemed much calmer now, as if he found the presence of the other horse reassuring. The girl's mare began to settle, too.

Sam looked around desperately. He had to find a way into the volcano! "Look," he said to the girl's back, "it's really important that I get inside the volcano's crater. Is there anyone in the village who knows a path that won't get me killed?"

The girl didn't turn around.

"It's urgent," Sam said. "I'm on a Quest!"

"You're in my way," the girl snapped, turning and brushing past Warrior to get to the other side of her mare. She leaned down to adjust the saddle's straps.

Anger flashed inside Sam. "Avantia is in danger," he cried. "You must help me!"

She looked at him over the saddle. "I must?" she said, her voice scathing. Her eyes travelled over him and she snorted. "I am Lara, daughter of Elkon, Chieftain of Stonewin. I do not take orders from anyone!"

Sam stared into her haughty face and decided he could not change her mind. He drew himself up. "Fine," he said icily. "Farewell."

He turned Warrior, thinking he would have to go back into the village and knock on every door until he found someone who could help him – if anyone even could.

"I did not give you permission to

leave, farm boy," Lara said behind him. Surprised, Sam wheeled Warrior back around to face her as the girl swung up into her saddle. Her bright eyes flashed at him through the gloom. "Although I do not have to help you, I have decided that I will."

Sam's anger melted into sudden hope. "You know someone who can show me a way into the crater?"

"Of course I do," Lara said. "Me."

Sam regarded her doubtfully. The girl carried no weapon that he could see, and her slender figure didn't seem to promise much physical strength. "But...we will face many dangers. Terrifying Beasts... evil magic...and the volcano itself..."

He expected Lara's face to pale, but instead she grinned. "All the better! A chieftain's daughter never shies away from danger!"

She patted her mare's neck. The animal's eyes no longer rolled, and she stood quietly even as the volcano emitted a terrible growl and the ground shook once more. "Good girl, Swift," Lara murmured. "This way, farm boy!" She wheeled Swift

around and rode toward the smoking, rumbling mountain.

Sam urged Warrior after her, but he wondered if he was doing the right thing in drawing someone else into danger.

Would Tom have done the same?

CHAPTER SEVEN

A FLOOD OF FIRE

"So once you've tamed Epos, you must ride her in combat against Ferno – and Maximus the wizard?" Lara said.

Sam glanced back at her, wondering is she believed everything he'd told her about his Quest.

Lara was staring at him through narrowed eyes. "If you're lying to me, farm boy, I will personally drag you back to Stonewin and have my father lock you up for wasting my time!"

"It's the truth," Sam said.

"Well, in that case..." Her expression softened. "Aren't you lucky to have met me?"

Despite himself, Sam laughed.

"There's our path," Lara said, pointing at what looked like a dry streambed furrowing the mountainside. They'd long since left Stonewin behind and had been climbing for some time. She turned Swift into the ditch, and Sam and Warrior followed. Brittle black rock crackled under the horses' hooves like ice. "Old lava," Lara explained. "It came out of the crater. If we follow it, and it will lead us back there."

Sam hoped she was right. *I have to trust her*, he thought. *After all, Lara's lived her whole life beside this volcano.*

They had not gone far when grey flakes began to fall from the clouds. At first Sam thought it was snow, but the flakes didn't melt when they landed on his face and hands. In fact, they were hot to the touch.

Ash, Sam realised.

As they rode on, the ash-fall thickened. Soon, Lara, Sam and the horses were all covered in a grey dust that drained the colour out of their clothing and hair. The higher they climbed, the thicker the ash fell. They were wrapped in deepening gloom and Sam had to keep his head down to make sure it didn't get in his eyes

Lara halted Swift. Sam rode up beside her. "What's wrong?" he asked.

"We may be on the wrong

path," Lara said. She caught Sam's doubtful look. "It's the ash," she said defensively. "All these pathways run into each other. In the ash, even I can take a wrong turn."

Sam looked around. Lightning flashed in the billowing clouds above them. In its glare, he saw the black rim of the crater high above. Their ditch led straight to it. "There it is!" he cried, relieved. "You did find the right path."

"I never doubted it," Lara said.

Sam laughed – until the mountain shook, harder than ever before. Up the gully, close to the rim of the crater, an enormous boulder flew through the air as if it had been flung by a giant slingshot. Bright orange lava spewed into the ditch and raced down the mountainside – straight

towards Sam and Lara!

Sam clung to Warrior's thick neck as his horse reared up in fear. Beside him, Lara was wrestling with Swift's reins.

"That way!" she cried, pointing left.

As Lara and Swift scampered up a narrow ravine, Sam struggled to turn Warrior, who was not as nimble. His horse reared up, hooves kicking the air, then galloped after Swift. Heat hit the back of Sam's head like a flaming fist. He glanced back to see lava pour down the ditch they had been in just moments before.

He halted Warrior beside Lara on the grey mountainside. They were all panting, the horses tossing their heads with fear. Even Lara's eyes were wide. The lava had formed a fiery river, sweeping away the rocks and bushes, the air above it shimmering with heat.

"That was close," Sam said.

"But we made it," Lara replied. Her face was streaked with ash and sweat, but she grinned, her teeth flashing white. She seemed more exhilarated than frightened, but her smile faded when a horrible yowling shattered the ash-filled air. "What's that?"

Sam twisted in the saddle, peering into the gloom.

Charging through the swirling ash came a small pack of ferocious-looking creatures. They were more than half his height, covered in shaggy fur, with sharp tusks curving at the corners of their snouts. Their

vicious claws scrabbled across the rocks.

"Warthogs!" Sam gasped.

A swirl of the wind brought him their scent even through the acrid smoke, and he gagged on the stench of rotting meat.

"They're heading straight for us!" cried Lara.

And then Sam heard a new voice – a mocking, sneering voice he remembered all too well.

"Of course they're heading for you, you stupid girl! I conjured them."

It was Maximus.

Over their heads, the ash swirled and thickened, forming the image of the evil Boy Wizard's face, turned blood-red by the glow of lava beneath.

"They will devour you where you

stand," Maximus said. "And so will
end Sam of Littleton's foolish Quest."
The giant face sneered. "You think
you're a match for Maximus, son of
Malvel? A pitiful farm boy, and the
daughter of a worthless chieftain of
a worthless town? Fools! You cannot
stop me. One by one, I will destroy
the Good Beasts of Avantia!"

The enormous face dissolved into swirling ash. Maximus's laughter echoed around the mountainside, mingling with the snarls of the warthogs.

Claws and teeth flashing, the ferocious creatures charged at Sam and Lara.

Sam drew his sword. "While my heart beats," he shouted, "I will defeat this evil!"

Battle was about to begin.

PART TWO

BATTLE IN THE SKIES

CHAPTER ONE

A FIGHT FOR SURVIVAL

Sam pulled the shield from his back and held it ready. His stomach churned and his heart pounded. These warthogs would be far more deadly than hyenas. *And I've only had a day's sword training!*

The nearest warthog launched itself straight at Warrior. Sam batted the flat of his blade against the warthog's

muzzle. It shrieked and skidded away,
blood streaming from its nose.

Sam couldn't believe how accurate
his attack had been. And then,
suddenly, he remembered that Daltec
had said the Golden Gauntlets gave
their wearer special sword skills. *As
long as I wear the gauntlet,* he thought,
I really can use a sword!

Another warthog leapt up at him,
saliva dripping from its snarling jaws.

Sam hammered the hilt of his sword onto its skull and the creature fell back and staggered away, yelping in pain.

A frightened whinny made Sam turn around. Swift's saddle was empty!

"Lara!" he cried. Then he saw her on the ground, scrabbling backwards as two drooling warthogs approached her, their tusks glowing red in the light of the lava. Sam drove Warrior towards the nearest one, and a flick of his blade sent it howling away. But the other warthog lowered its head and charged. "Lara!" Sam shouted again. "Look out!"

His heart was pounding. *I'll never reach her in time!*

But even as the warthog rushed her, Lara twisted to grab the branch

of a dead bush. She broke it off
with a snap, and thrust it into the
approaching lava. The tip of the
branch burst into flame. She swung
the branch like a club, striking the
face of the oncoming warthog with
a shower of sparks. The animal
squealed and scurried away, smoke
trailing from its burning whiskers.

Out of the corner of his eye, Sam
saw another warthog charging. He
spun Warrior, and his brave horse
reared fearlessly, kicking out his
massive forehooves. The charging
warthog tumbled away, rolling over
and over. Then it righted itself. With
a snarl, it prowled towards Lara.

Flames licked along Lara's branch,
almost reaching her fingers, and she
tossed it aside. Sam gasped. *She's
unarmed!*

But Sam's new friend drew out a
long silver dagger from the pocket of
her green cloak. She held it in both
hands and pointed it at the charging
creature. The animal skidded to avoid
her blade. Its front legs buckled and it
gave a squeal as it slammed face-first
onto the ground.

"Where did you get that dagger?"
Sam called.

Lara shrugged. "A chieftain's daughter is always prepared!" Then her eyes widened. "Behind you!"

Sam twisted in the saddle and flung up his shield, just as another warthog leapt up at him. Though it remained as light as a feather on Sam's arm, the shield's surface turned to black rock. The warthog slammed into it. The impact almost knocked Sam from the saddle, and he gripped Warrior's reins. The warthog dropped to the ground and lay still.

The remaining animals seemed to lose the will to fight. They turned tail and scampered away, disappearing into the grey haze of ash, leaving behind only marks on the ground and pitiful whines in the air.

Exhilarated, Sam sheathed his sword. "Well done," he said.

"Between the two of us, those warthogs didn't stand a chance!"

"Your skills with that sword aren't bad," Lara said. "Maybe you are training to be a Knight, after all." She smiled, and Sam grinned too.

"We'd better hurry," Sam said, glancing up at the crater rim. "The volcano may not be done with us yet."

Lara nodded. "Maximus may not be done with us yet, either!"

She climbed back onto Swift and they resumed the trek up the mountainside. To their right, lava continued to pour down the gully. Sam pointed at the river of molten rock. "We can't follow that into the crater."

"There's another way," Lara said, pointing. Sam followed her outstretched finger and saw a column of black, glassy rock thrusting up beside the gaping mouth of a tunnel. They rode up to it in silence. Hot wind roared out of the tunnel as though it were the mouth of a giant, angry monster. A red light flickered in the depths.

Sam glanced at Lara. "In there?"

"Yes," she confirmed, her face looking pale in the semi-darkness.

Sam swallowed. *I can't turn back*, he thought. *Whatever dangers lie ahead, I must face them. Otherwise, Avantia is doomed...*

He slipped down from Warrior, and tied the horse's reins to a branch of a dead bush sprouting forlornly from the parched earth. Lara did the same with Swift.

Then Sam took a deep breath and

drew his sword. Gripping it tightly, he began, "You don't have to—"

Lara drew her own slender dagger. "We're a team," she said.

Sam smiled, grateful to have made such an ally...and friend. "Thank you," he said, staring back into the gaping black mouth of the tunnel. "Let's go."

They stepped into the tunnel. Black, glassy rock lined the walls, reflecting back the heat from the burning wind blowing in their faces. They quickly left behind the gloomy light from outside, but they weren't in darkness – orange and red light flickered ahead of them, casting confusing reflections and flickering shadows across the shining stone.

"It's hot enough to bake bread in here," Sam muttered.

Stinging sweat from his forehead ran into Sam's eyes. His whole body prickled with the heat. Beside him, the red light made the sweat on Lara's face glisten, and turned the blade of her dagger the colour of blood.

The flickering light drew nearer, and they emerged from the tunnel onto a wide ledge. It jutted out above a vast pool of lava that bubbled and seethed beneath them. The heat hit Sam like a hammer blow.

We're inside the crater! he thought.

The ledge ran all around the fiery cavern, just below the rim. Off to his right, lava poured out through an opening in the crater wall. Sam guessed it must lead to the ditch they'd been following up the mountain.

But as he stared into that vast sea of molten rock, he realised something important was missing: Epos, the Flame Bird.

Then he felt Lara pulling at his sleeve. He followed her gaze upward – and saw his quarry at last.

Hovering high above the pool of lava was the most beautiful and magnificent creature that Sam

could imagine. Her vast wings
blocked out the billowing, lightning-
shot clouds of smoke and ash, yellow

flames rippling across feathers of beaten gold and glinting off her razor-sharp talons.

Epos!

CHAPTER TWO

INSIDE THE FLAME BIRD'S LAIR

Epos's curved beak opened and she unleashed a furious scream – as if she were outraged that two such insignificant creatures had penetrated her lair. It was even louder than the volcano's roar.

"What now?" Lara shouted to Sam.

Sam shook his head. "I don't know!"

"She sounds angry," Lara said. "Is she angry with us?"

"I don't think so," Sam replied. "The volcano started erupting long before we arrived..."

The realisation hit Sam like a splash of icy water. *Maximus! As well as conjuring those warthogs, he must have used his dark magic to unsettle the volcano...and infuriate Epos. He wants her angry, so that when he arrives with Ferno, she'll fight the dragon to the death!*

Sam's head shot up when he heard a whooshing roar rise above the volcano's constant rumble. A giant fireball had formed between Epos's front talons, writhing like a stream of flowing water. And then, with a sharp, vicious motion, the Flame Bird hurled the fireball straight at them.

"Take cover!" Sam yelled. Lara

ducked behind him as he raised his
shield. He was only just in time. The
surface turned to ice as the fireball
struck, snuffing out the flame in a
huge cloud of steam. The shield rang
as though it had been hit with a giant
hammer, and Sam staggered back.
He crashed into Lara, sending her
sprawling onto the ledge. Her dagger
fell from her hand and skittered
towards the crater.

Sam lunged forwards and snatched

the weapon before it could fall. He passed it back to his friend.

"Thanks," Lara said. Her eyes widened as she stared at Epos. "Though I don't think my dagger will be much use here."

The Beast was creating a second fireball.

Lara's right, Sam thought. *We can't fight Epos. So how can I calm this Beast?*

Epos hurled her fireball. Sam braced himself for the impact, his shield raised, but again he was sent staggering back by the force of its strike. He recovered and ran towards the edge of the rock shelf, but the Flame Bird screamed and wheeled away to a different part of the crater. A third fireball grew between her talons.

Sam and Lara were driven back toward the tunnel, as fireball followed fireball. Sam could get no closer to Epos, whose shrieks and screams grew angrier. *She's not giving up*, Sam thought desperately. And sooner or later—

"Look out!" Lara yelled, and Sam saw that the Flame Bird had conjured her largest fireball yet.

The monstrous globe of flame hurtled toward them. Gasping, Sam crouched in front of Lara and raised the shield once more, hoping that its magic was powerful enough to fend off...

The massive fireball slammed into the shield, exploding into sparks and steam against the icy surface. The force blasted both Sam and Lara backwards into the hot stone wall behind them. Bruised and aching, Sam staggered back to his feet. Lara pushed herself up. Her forehead was bleeding, and she wiped it angrily with the back of her hand.

"This isn't working," Lara said. "How can we tame the Beast when we can't get near her?"

Sam stared up at Epos. The giant fireball seemed to have taken all the Flame Bird's strength for the moment. Now she circled the crater, like a bird whose nest had been disturbed.

Lara's right, Sam thought. He remembered how he had first seen her, standing close to Swift's head, murmuring into the frightened mare's twitching ear. *The only way to tame any Beast – magical or not – is to get close. I have to convince it I mean no harm. Which means I have no choice but to…*

Sam took off his shield and laid it on the rock. Then he sheathed his sword and unbuckled his belt, laying them on top of the shield.

"What are you doing?" Lara asked, looking stunned.

"What's necessary," Sam told her. Heart thumping, he strode to the lip of the ledge. He held his hands out in front of him, palms up, fingers spread, to show he was unarmed.

And helpless, he thought, as Epos cocked one burning-bright eye at him. She circled lower, a new fireball forming between her talons.

Sam swallowed hard, and called. "Epos! I am not your enemy. I need your help!"

Epos cocked her head the other way, and then swooped down, coming to a stop just in front of him. Her ruby-red eyes, glowing with internal fire, seemed to peer right into

his mind. He held his breath, awed,
frightened – and exhilarated. *She's
amazing!*

The fireball faded away. Epos gave a
low, questioning cry, and Sam's heart

leaped again, but this time with hope. He took a cautious step forward.

"Sam, be careful!" Lara said behind him.

"I will," he murmured back, taking one more step, so that he stood on the very lip of the ledge. There was nothing beyond his toes but a sheer drop right down into boiling lava. The Golden Gauntlet on his left hand tingled, an echo of the power that had filled Sam when he'd first put it on. Epos moved even closer, the wind from her wings buffeting him. He spread his legs wider to steady himself.

Epos stretched out her head towards him. The phoenix's shining gold beak looked sharp enough to cut him in two with a single bite. But strangely, Sam didn't feel afraid. He reached out his gauntleted hand to touch it.

Swift and bright as lightning, white light exploded all around him, driving away the red glow of the lava, turning the billowing clouds of ash high above the colour of snow.

"Sam!" Lara cried. "You're... glowing!"

Sam looked down and gasped. It was true! Light poured out of his skin, shining through his clothes. He glowed so brightly, he could hardly look at himself! A strong tingle surged up inside him, flooding his heart and head. He felt the power race down his arm, into and through the gauntlet, and into the beak of the Beast.

The white light vanished. The tingling ceased. But suddenly Sam felt a presence in his mind, thoughts that weren't his own... They were the thoughts of Epos the Flame Bird!

Yes, Epos told him. *I will fight with you, Sam of Littleton.*

Sam suddenly realised he'd been holding his breath. He let it out in a sigh of triumph and relief. He'd done it!

He'd tamed the Flame Bird!

CHAPTER THREE

EPOS TAKES FLIGHT

Epos was perched calmly on the ledge, preening her golden feathers with her razor-sharp beak. Sam and Lara sat together beside her huge talons, examining the magical map. The icon of Epos was right where it always had been: the crater of the volcano.

But the icon of Ferno was moving northeast from his mountain lair –

straight towards them.

"In Stonewin, the people know how to survive an eruption," Lara said in a worried voice, tracing the dragon's path with her finger. "But an eruption *and* a dragon? If Ferno attacks the town—"

"We can't let that happen," Sam agreed. "Epos and I will intercept him before he gets to Stonewin." He put a hand on the Flame Bird's talon and she reached down, ruffling his hair with her massive beak.

Lara got to her feet. "Thank you," she said. "But I must warn my father all the same."

"Take the horses," Sam said. "Ride back to the village. Tell your people what's about to happen."

Lara nodded. She ran to the tunnel, but at its mouth she stopped and glanced back. "Be careful," she said. Then she smiled. "And good luck, farm boy."

Sam grinned back. "You too, chieftain's daughter."

With a quick wave of farewell, Lara dashed into the darkness.

Sam glanced up at Epos. "We have to stop Maximus and Ferno," he said.

Of course. Even Epos's thoughts felt fiery, as though they were burning inside Sam's brain. Spreading her wings, she flattened her body to the hot stone ledge.

Sam took hold of her shining golden feathers, soft as silk but warm to the touch. *This is amazing,* he thought. He hesitated only for an instant before swinging his right leg over her neck. He held on tightly as she straightened – and his stomach leapt into his mouth as she launched them both into empty space.

Epos rose out of the crater, beating her powerful wings. Avoiding the towering plumes of smoke and ash, she banked sharply left. Far below, Sam saw Lara as she mounted Swift. She leant low, saying something. An instant later the mare took off at a gallop down the mountain, with Warrior pounding behind. The horses dwindled away beneath Sam as Epos beat her wings again and again, lifting higher into a sky that was still bright, even though the sun had fallen almost to the horizon.

Sam found himself grinning as the air whipped through his hair and clothes. He stared in amazement at the ground far below. Farms, fields and villages formed a green and gold

patchwork, seamed by roads, alive
with tiny figures of people working
in the fields. Up and up they flew,
until he was glad of the furnace-like
heat coming off the bird, to protect
him from the chill wind streaming
past. They soared through a small
white cloud, and Sam whooped as it

engulfed him for a moment. "I always wondered what it would feel like to touch a cloud!" he shouted above the wind. In his mind he could feel Epos's warm amusement.

Sam glanced back, past Epos's streaming tail. They still had not flown as high as the towering cloud of ash that spewed from the volcano, but at least they had left it far behind. Sam carefully let go of Epos's feathers, gripping the bird's back only with his knees, just as he did astride Warrior. He took out and unrolled the map.

Epos's icon was now far west of both the volcano and Stonewin. Sam peered closer. There! Ferno's image was nearing a large patch of blue: a lake. A perfect place for a battle involving fire.

"Epos!" Sam called. "If we turn

east now, we can meet Ferno over that big lake! That way, we won't hurt anyone on the ground!"

Yes, Epos answered. She banked right. Sam spotted the glittering silvery surface of the lake. He grasped Epos's feathers once more and urged the great Beast to fly even faster. As the wind screamed in his ears, he bent low over the Flame Bird's back, exhilaration mingling with growing fear. He was about to face an evil Boy Wizard, and a Fire Dragon, in battle. The fate of all Avantia rested on his shoulders...

Epos screamed, and a name tore through Sam's head like a burst of flame.

Ferno!

Sam squinted, and a moment later he too saw the great Beast. From this distance, Ferno appeared to be as small as a bat, but he swelled with alarming speed to become a vast, dark shape. His black scales glittered in the lowering sun, while his massive teeth and curved claws shone an eerie shade of white. Astride the mighty dragon, Sam saw a tiny human figure…

Maximus…
The Battle of the Beasts was about
to begin!

CHAPTER FOUR

FIRE IN THE SKY

How dare this boy turn Ferno to evil!

Epos's words burned in Sam's mind
like glowing lava from her volcano.
Her fury was so pure that Sam felt
it as strongly as if it were his own.

Ferno swept closer. Sam could
see Maximus clearly now, mounted
in a saddle of black, silver-studded
leather that was bound tightly around
Ferno's torso by a thick leather

strap. A mocking sneer curled the Boy Wizard's thin lips. His right hand, encased in the stolen Golden Gauntlet, gripped the handle of a long whip. Black flames flickered and crackled as he snapped it across Ferno's heaving flank. Ferno roared in pain and fury, but redoubled his efforts, speeding even faster towards Epos and Sam.

How could he have turned a Good Beast evil so easily? Sam wondered.

"Give up, you fool!" Maximus shouted scornfully as the two Beasts closed to within a hundred paces. "You cannot hope to overcome the full might of Maximus and Ferno. Even if you knock me from Ferno's back, I can save myself with my dark magic – unlike you!" He pointed down at the lake far below. "Jump!

If you are fortunate, you might
survive the fall!"

"Never!" Sam yelled. All his doubts
were forgotten, all his fear swallowed
up by anger and determination.
I might not win – but I can die trying!

With a growl of fury, Maximus

again cracked his fiery whip against Ferno's side. The two Beasts closed the short distance that remained with blinding speed, slamming together like mountains colliding. Sam had to grab two handfuls of Epos's feathers to stop himself from falling off the Beast's neck.

Ferno's giant jaws snapped and slavered at Epos, who fought him off with her slashing beak. They grappled and clawed with their enormous talons. Sam saw golden feathers fluttering away in the wind, while black scales fell like strange rain towards the lake, far below.

The Beasts are tearing each other apart!

While the Beasts struggled, Maximus swung his burning whip at Sam. Sam's shield turned to ice as the whip snapped across it. The fiery rope slid harmlessly away in a cloud of steam.

Up! Sam willed Epos, and the Flame Bird untangled herself from Ferno,

beating her enormous wings and driving them high above the roaring dragon and its cursing rider.

As they hovered, Sam stared down into the dragon's enormous eyes, each almost as large as Sam's magical shield. From the picture in *The Complete Book of Beasts*, Sam knew they should have looked like molten copper. Instead, they were the colour of coal, wreathed in black fire. *Maximus's enchantment must run deep*, he thought.

Ferno's terrifying mouth gaped open, and an enormous stream of fire tore through the air. Sam jerked violently away from the vicious heat. He could smell something burning, and when he raised a hand to his head a clump of charred, blackened hair came away in his fingers.

Epos pulled out of her dive, Sam's breath whooshing out as he was slammed against her back. He grabbed her feathers more tightly as she flew skywards again. Ferno roared and raced towards her.

Down! Sam commanded, and Epos dropped like a boulder again, her talons closing around Ferno's horns. She twisted the dragon's head this way and that. Ferno roared in helpless fury. As Epos snapped at her foe, quick as a striking snake, Sam was almost unseated. He clung to her neck as though she were a wild, bucking horse.

But the buffeting stopped as Ferno suddenly reared up to slash at Epos with his talons, and Sam straightened. "I need to get to Maximus!" he cried. Epos turned her flank toward the

dragon and beat her wings hard,
driving her body into Ferno's side.

Suddenly, Sam found himself sitting
directly across from the Boy Wizard,
whose eyes widened in surprise. Sam
swung his shield. Its silver surface

turned instantly to black rock as Sam
drove it into the other boy's arm.
Maximus was knocked half-out of
his saddle. His frantic, flailing hand
caught a flapping leather rein at the
last instant.

"Get away from them!" Maximus
yelled. But Ferno didn't seem to
hear – or he was too angry to listen
to his rider. He stayed close to Epos,

snarling and snapping.

One more blow will knock Maximus right off Ferno's back, Sam thought.

"Closer!" he urged Epos, feeling a thrill of excitement. Maximus was tangled in the leather strap. He was there for the taking.

But the Fire Dragon lashed his tail into Epos's flank.

"Argh!" Sam yelped, as the Flame Bird lurched to the left. Sam's stomach flipped as the world turned upside down. He tried desperately to cling onto the Flame Bird's feathers, but it was no use.

With a cry of terror, he fell.

The world whirled crazily as he plummeted – but instead of the hard, rocky ground, Sam felt the warmth of Epos's feathers. The Flame Bird had swooped down to give him a soft

landing! Sam caught a handful of
feathers in his gauntleted hand, and
pulled himself tight against Epos's
back again.

You saved my life, Epos, he thought.
No one could have survived that fall.

Then a thought lit up in his head
like a beacon in the night. Maximus

had boasted that even if he fell from the dragon's back, he could save himself. So why had he seemed so determined to hang onto the Fire Dragon? Could a fall mean that Maximus would lose his magical control of Ferno? Without his rider's evil commands, the Good Beast would stop attacking Epos.

Whoever makes his opponent fall wins this battle, Sam thought. *But how can I knock Maximus out of his saddle without harming Ferno?*

CHAPTER FIVE

DISARMED

Sam felt a fierce heat rising from below. Looking down, he saw a spinning sphere of orange and red flame growing between Epos's talons. From far below, Ferno rose up toward her. With a shriek, she hurled the fireball at Maximus, who flattened himself against Ferno's back as the fireball passed over him, exploding and raining a shower of sparks over the lake.

But Maximus had not been quite fast enough. Sam grinned as he saw the Boy Wizard roll around on the dragon's back, yelping in pain as he beat at his singed hair.

Ferno kept climbing, closer and closer, and Maximus shook his fist at Sam and Epos. "Burn them!" Maximus shouted, and Ferno raised his head to spit a stream of flame.

"Dodge right!" Sam yelled. Epos folded her wings and sideslipped, but the flame tore through the tip of her tail, sending her spinning. As half a dozen golden feathers vanished in a puff of black smoke, Sam felt Epos's pain like a red-hot poker in his head. Half-blinded by the agony, he held on for dear life as, shrieking, Epos fell into a spiralling, fluttering descent.

He raised streaming eyes just as

another blast of dragon fire rushed
past. It missed Epos, but tore into the
pine forest on the lake's northern
shore. Trees exploded into flame
below them, fire and smoke billowing
into the sky. For the first time, Sam
felt fear coming from Epos. *I may not
be able to pull up,* she thought. *Hold on,
Sam of Littleton!*

The swirling air buffeted him. Once

again he lost his grip, and almost
slid off Epos's left side, but a gentle
bat of her wing sent him sprawling
across her back. He grabbed a
gauntleted handful of feathers and
worked his way, bit by bit, back up
toward his perch on Epos's neck. He
could feel the Flame Bird's intense
concentration, could sense her trying
to judge the wind and her speed
just right...

Then she snapped her wings out
straight, gliding at exhilarating speed
through the acrid, choking smoke
that billowed from the burning forest.
Sam dared to let go with his right
hand and twisted around. Behind,
he saw Ferno bearing down on them,
jaws gaping to unleash yet more
flame.

"Turn left!" he called, and Epos

obeyed instantly. The dragon's fire slashed past on their right, igniting more treetops, but the phoenix had banked so sharply that Sam was again thrown hard to the side. For a terrifying moment he hung almost upside-down, clinging on to her feathers with his left hand to keep himself from plunging to his death.

Amid the chaos of the world whirling all around him, he caught a glint of shining steel. His precious sword was slipping from its scabbard! Before he could snatch at it with his free hand, the blade was gone, spinning and flipping before splashing into the shallows of the lake.

Heavy dread filled Sam. How could he possibly defeat Maximus now?

Gulping air, Sam hauled himself onto Epos's back once more. A flicker

of movement caught the corner of his vision and he twisted his head to see Ferno diving out of the sky, a vast winged shadow with Maximus astride his neck. The Boy Wizard, face twisted with hatred, whirled his flaming black whip over his head.

"No magic, no sword — no hope!" Maximus yelled. "Goodbye, so-called hero of Avantia!"

"Dive!" Sam urged Epos. The phoenix was smaller and more agile than Ferno. If they dived low to the lake, the dragon might have to pull up before—

But Sam's half-formed strategy vanished from his mind when he saw someone splashing out of the shallow water below, a sword – *his* sword – in her hands.

Lara!

CHAPTER SIX

THE FINAL FALL

"Lower!" Sam shouted to Epos.
"Lower!"

The great bird dropped like a rock
toward the beach. As Sam had hoped,
Ferno followed, but then pulled up short
and wheeled up into the sky again.

"Coward!" Sam heard Maximus
screaming at the dragon.

Sam's heart leapt into his throat as
the lakeshore rushed up at him, and

he gasped when, at the last second,
the great feathered wings snapped
open. The abrupt halt flung Sam hard
against Epos's hot feathered back,
and then they were on the ground.
Lara rushed up to meet them. In the
bushes behind her, Warrior and Swift
reared and whinnied.

"What are you doing here?" Sam cried.

Lara grinned. "Saving your neck!"

She tossed the sword to him hilt first and he caught it neatly. "You didn't really think I was going to cower in Stonewin once I'd warned them about Ferno, did you? There's too much fun to miss out on."

She fell silent as a dark shadow passed over their heads. They both looked up.

"Ferno's coming!" Sam said, as Lara scrambled away towards where the horses stood, in the thick copse of bushes.

Sam grabbed hold of Epos's neck feathers. "Up!" he cried, and the Flame Bird powered into the air. She banked hard left, swung around in a tight circle, and met the onrushing Fire Dragon head-on. They crashed together like colliding boulders, twisting around and around each other, striking with teeth and claws. Sam yelled in triumph as Epos's talons closed on Ferno's tail, then gasped as Ferno snapped his head around and clamped his jaws onto Epos's feathered shoulder. The phoenix shrieked in agony.

Once again, the Beasts' struggles brought Sam and Maximus close together.

"Die, fool!" Maximus yelled. His gauntleted hand flicked his black, flaming whip.

Sam ducked and struck out with his sword. The skill of his own gauntlet enabled him to bat the whip aside, but its smoking tail sliced through the skin of his arm, making him cry out in pain.

Maximus drew back his arm for another blow, but this time Sam was able to meet it with his magical shield, hoisting up a wall of white ice for the whip to strike. Maximus's weapon recoiled, its snake-like length hissing as it turned its ferocity on the Boy Wizard.

In terror, Maximus raised both hands to protect his face, releasing his grip on the saddle – and in that moment, the Beasts broke free of each other with a mighty heave. Ferno rolled, unseating Maximus from the saddle. Sam's enemy only just managed to grab onto a leather strap, but could do nothing to stop his whip tumbling away through the air. Groaning with the effort, he started pulling himself hand over hand back toward his seat – where he would have control of Ferno again.

"Closer!" Sam yelled to Epos. The Flame Bird lunged at Ferno with a

battle cry. As their flanks slammed
into each other, Sam reached out as
far as he could with the sword. With
a flick of his wrist, he sliced through
the saddle's strap.

Maximus could do nothing as
both he and his saddle slid down
the dragon's scaly body. He plunged

towards the burning forest and vanished beneath the thick floor of grey smoke.

Ferno broke away from Epos. He dived, wheeled, and swung back toward Sam and the Flame Bird. Sam readied his sword, but he lowered it when he saw that Ferno's eyes were no longer black. They gleamed gold.

Maximus's spell over the dragon had been broken!

Epos landed right at the edge of the lake, her talons sending up sprays of water. Lara cantered up on Swift, with Warrior galloping behind.

"You did it!" she shouted, bringing Swift to a stop.

"*We* did it," Sam corrected her. "I wouldn't even have got into the crater if you hadn't showed me the way. And if you hadn't retrieved my sword..."

"Who am I to argue?" Lara said. She punched the air. "We did it!"

Sam slipped off Epos's back and slid down her wing. Warrior trotted over, and he hugged the big horse's neck.

Ferno landed beside Epos, hot wind blasting around Sam and Warrior. The Fire Dragon looked at Sam with his whirling copper eyes, and then dropped his enormous head to the ground in

a gesture of thanks and respect. Sam stretched up and touched the scaly muzzle, awed by the enormous power both Beasts possessed.

Epos's fiery thoughts filled Sam's head. *Thank you, Sam*, she told him. *You are a true hero of Avantia.*

Sam grinned. "You're very welcome," he replied.

CHAPTER SEVEN

A HERO OF AVANTIA

Sam turned away from Epos and went over to where Lara was waiting with Warrior and Swift.

"We should go and look for Maximus," he said.

Lara blinked in surprise. "But surely he couldn't survive that fall," Lara said.

"He's a wizard," Sam said grimly.

"He could have used his magic to escape. And who knows what he might try next?" He raised his left hand. "Besides, he still has the other Golden Gauntlet. It belongs to Tom, Master of the Beasts. We need to get it back!"

"That makes sense," Lara admitted. She slid down from Swift. "You two stay here," she told the horses, and they calmly trotted over to a patch of grass and began to graze.

Sword in hand and shield settled firmly on his forearm, Sam led Lara into the smouldering woods. Moss grew thickly on the trunks and the ground squelched under their feet. *Good thing the forest is so wet*, Sam thought. *The fire couldn't take hold.* Even so, here and there trees and logs sputtered and hissed and flickered flame, and smoke drifted through the trees in long grey tendrils. Sam cautiously stepped around hot spots, clouds of ash rising around his boots.

They didn't have to search long. Maximus stood in a clearing not a hundred paces into the forest, stamping out flames that flickered along the edge of his cape, which he had flung to the ground.

Sword outstretched, Sam stepped into the clearing. Out of the corner of his eye, he saw the gleam of Lara's dagger. "It's over, Maximus," he said. "You're coming back to the palace as my prisoner."

"Over?" Soot streaked Maximus's face, but scorn glittered in his eyes. "It's just beginning. I still have this…" He clenched his right hand into a golden fist. Black flames flickered across the knuckles of the gauntlet. "I can still control the Beasts. This was just the first battle in a very long war. And when I win, Avantia will fall! Take that message back to the palace, if you like. But you will never take me!"

Sam started forwards, but he had not taken two steps when Maximus flicked his hand, conjuring black

lightning from his fingertips.

And then he was gone, leaving behind just a small cloud of smoke where he had been standing.

"Now what?" asked Lara.

Sam sighed and sheathed his sword. "I must return to the palace at once, and warn Tom and Elenna that Maximus is still at large...and still has the Golden Gauntlet."

They returned to the horses and the Beasts. Lara went straight to Swift and swung up astride her. She glanced at Ferno. "I'll go back to Stonewin and tell my father we needn't fear the dragon," she said.

"I think you can tell him not to fear the volcano, either," Sam said. "Now that we've won the battle, I don't think Epos will make it erupt."

Lara nodded. "Thank you for the

adventure," she said. "The next time you have a Quest, look for me in Stonewin."

And then she galloped away on Swift.

Many hours later, as the sun was setting, Sam and Warrior finally rode up to King Hugo's palace. Sam's fellow recruits ran out from the gates to meet him, followed by Daltec, Tom and Elenna.

The recruits shouted with amazement at the sight of Epos and Ferno. The two Beasts had escorted Sam across the kingdom, and now hovered overhead.

Tom strode to the head of the greeting party. He took Warrior's bridle and grinned up at Sam.

"You did it! You fulfilled your Quest!"

"I couldn't have done it without help," Sam said, though his heart swelled with pride. "A girl from Stonewin came with me."

Tom laughed and shot a glance at a smiling Elenna. "In my experience, Sam, whenever a true friend shows up to help you with your Quest, it's a sure sign you're going to succeed!"

With a mighty rush of wind, Epos and Ferno landed nearby. The recruits crowded around them.

"I can't believe how big they are!"

"Can she really make fireballs?"

"Look at those eyes!"

"Never mind the eyes, look at those claws!"

Sam slid down from Warrior and went over to Epos. The phoenix reached out and rubbed her beak

on his shoulder. He could no longer
hear her thoughts, he realized with
a pang of sadness, but he supposed
he didn't need to hear them now. He
knew what the Beast was saying.

He reached up and rubbed her beak.
"Goodbye, Epos," he said. "And thank
you."

Epos let out a gentle squawk before

she and Ferno spread their enormous wings and leaped together into the air. In moments, the Beasts were only tiny specks in the orange sky. They circled once then separated, Ferno flying south and Epos east, back toward their homes.

The golden gauntlet Sam had worn for so long, which had seemed as light as a second skin, suddenly felt as heavy as lead. It dragged at his arm as though it would pull his hand right off. Groaning, he freed his hand from it. In his grasp, it felt dull and dead, empty of its tingling power. Sam turned to Daltec and held it out. "Someone else will need this soon."

Tom frowned. "How so?" he asked.

"Maximus still has the other gauntlet," Sam replied.

Tom raised his eyes and stared

after the departing Beasts for a long moment. Then he glanced around at all the recruits. "Maximus should be worried," he said, his grin returning. "We have a whole academy of heroes ready and willing to face him!"

The recruits cheered.

"Now, back into the palace, everyone," Tom cried. "We must have a feast to celebrate Sam's Quest!"

The recruits cheered again, and streamed back toward the gates. The guard who had met Sam on his arrival at the palace just two days before stepped forward to take Warrior back to the stables.

Sam turned toward the east, hoping for one last glimpse of Epos. He couldn't see her, but as he peered up into the fading sky, something fluttered out of the air right at his feet.

He bent over and picked up a
feather, enormous, smooth, golden –
and still a little warm from the heat
of Epos's body. He ran it between
his fingers, marvelling at its silky
smoothness. Then he tucked it
carefully into the leather pouch
on his belt.

I'll send it in a scroll back to Lisbeth,

he thought. His big sister would never believe the adventure he'd had.

"Sam! You're going to miss the feast!"

Sam turned to see Zora and Will waiting for him at the archway into the palace.

He laughed and started running over to his friends. "I never miss a feast!"

Join a new hero on the next
Battle of the Beasts

TAGUS vs AMICTUS

Win an exclusive
Beast Quest T-shirt and goody bag!

In every Beast Quest book the Beast Quest logo is
hidden in one of the pictures. Find the logo in this book
and make a note of which page it appears on.
Send the page number in to us.
Each month we will draw one winner to receive
a Beast Quest T-shirt and goody bag.
Send your entry on a postcard listing the title of the
book and the number to:

THE BEAST QUEST COMPETITION:
Battle of the Beasts: Ferno versus Epos
Orchard Books
338 Euston Road, London NW1 3BH
Australian readers should email:
childrens.books@hachette.com.au

New Zealand readers should write to:
Beast Quest Competition
4 Whetu Place, Mairangi Bay, Auckland, NZ
or email: childrensbooks@hachette.co.nz

Only one entry per child.
Final draw: July 2013

You can also enter this competition
via the Beast Quest website: www.beastquest.co.uk

Join the Quest,
Join the Tribe

www.beastquest.co.uk

Have you checked out the Beast Quest website?
It's the place to go for games, downloads, activities,
sneak previews and lots of fun!

You can read all about your favourite Beasts, download free screensavers and desktop wallpapers for
your computer, and even challenge your friends
to a Beast Tournament.

Sign up to the newsletter at www.beastquest.co.uk
to receive exclusive extra content and the opportunity to enter special members-only competitions.
We'll send you up-to-date info on all the Beast
Quest books, including the next exciting series
which features six brand-new Beasts!

Get 30% off all Beast Quest Books at www.beastquest.co.uk
Enter the code BEAST at the checkout.

All books priced at £4.99.
Special bumper editions priced at £5.99.

Orchard Books are available from all good bookshops, or can
be ordered from our website: www.orchardbooks.co.uk,
or telephone 01235 827702, or fax 01235 8227703.

FREE COLLECTOR CARDS INSIDE!

Series 11: THE NEW AGE
COLLECT THEM ALL!

A new land, a deadly enemy and six new Beasts await Tom on his next adventure!

978 1 40831 841 6

978 1 40831 842 3

978 1 40831 843 0

978 1 40831 844 7

978 1 40831 845 4

978 1 40831 846 1

Series 12: THE DARKEST HOUR
Out January 2013

Meet six terrifying new Beasts!

Solak, Scourge of the Sea
Kajin the Beast Catcher
Issrilla the Creeping Menace
Vigrash the Clawed Eagle
Mirka the Ice Horse
Kama the Faceless Beast

**Watch out for the next
Special Bumper
Edition
OUT MARCH 2013!**

OUT NOVEMBER 2012!

MEET A NEW HERO OF AVANTIA

Dark magic has been unleashed!

Evil boy-Wizard Maximus is using the stolen golden gauntlet to wreak havoc on Avantia. A new hero must stand up to him, and battle the Beasts!

Join Tom on his Beast Quests
and take part in a terrifying adventure
where YOU call the shots!